ELIVIA SAVADIER

TIME TO GET
DRESSED!

A NEAL PORTER BOOK
ROARING BROOK PRESS
NEW MILFORD, CONNECTICUT

For Jane Feder

Copyright © 2006 by Elivia Savadier
A Neal Porter Book
Published by Roaring Brook Press
Roaring Brook Press is a division of Holtzbrinck Publishing Holdings Limited Partnership
143 West Street, New Milford, Connecticut 06776

Distributed in Canada by H. B. Fenn and Company Ltd.

Library of Congress Cataloging-in-Publication Data:
Savadier, Elivia.
Time to get dressed! / by Elivia Savadier. — 1st ed.
p. cm.
"A Neal Porter Book."
Summary: While time flies by on a busy morning, Solomon is determined to dress himself,
but his father intervenes and all goes smoothly — for a while.
[1. Clothing and dress — Fiction.   2. Individuality — Fiction.   3. Fathers and sons — Fiction.
4. Time — Fiction.]   I. Title
PZ7.S2584Tim 2006   [E] — dc22   2005019923
ISBN-13: 978-1-59643-161-4
ISBN-10: 1-59643-161-X

Roaring Brook Press books are available for special promotions and premiums.
For details contact: Director of Special Markets, Holtzbrinck Publishers.

First edition April 2006
Printed in China
2   4   6   8   10   9   7   5   3   1

Solomon likes to dress himself.

Me!

Solomon puts on his **shirt**.

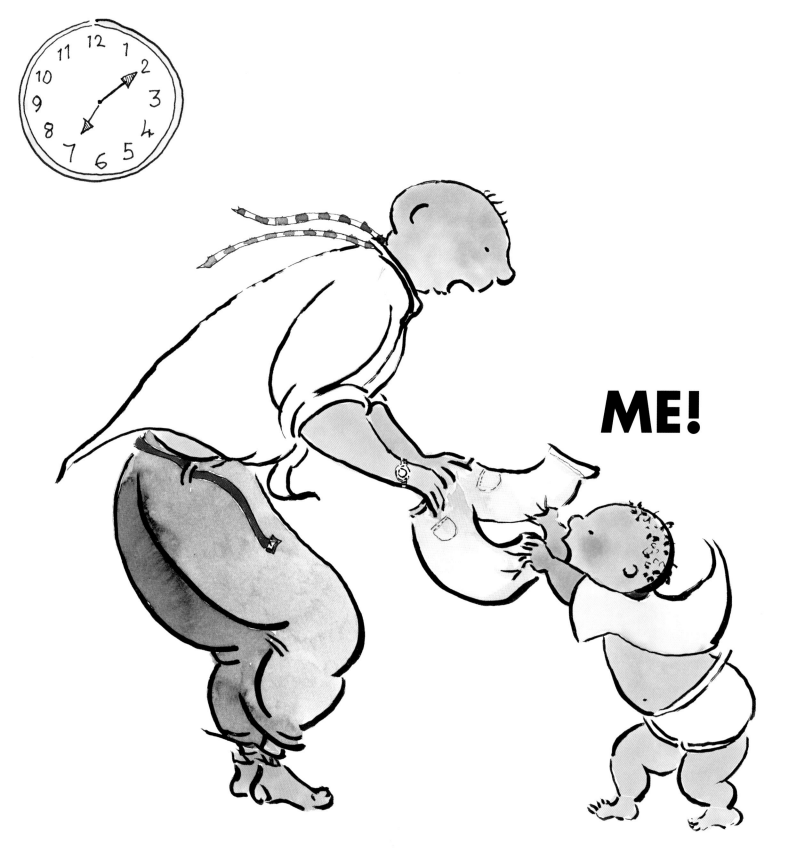

Solomon puts on his **pants**.

Solomon puts on his **sock**.

ME!

Solomon puts on his **shoe**.

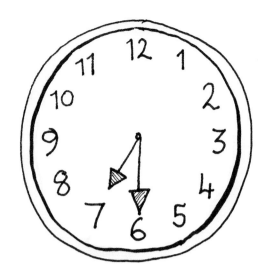

Now it's getting late,
so when the big hand is on the **six**
and the little hand is on the **seven** . . .

Daddy says,

Daddy helps Solomon put on his **shirt**.

Daddy helps Solomon put on his **pants**.

Daddy helps Solomon put on his **socks**.

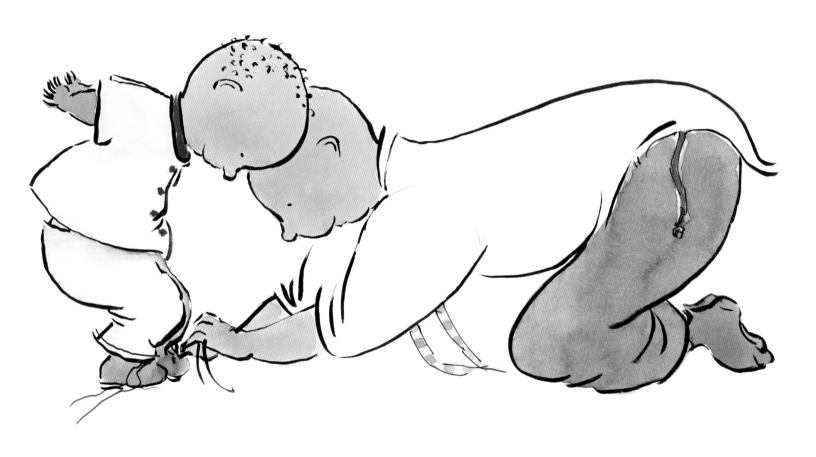

Daddy helps Solomon put on his **shoes**.

Now it's time for breakfast. Solomon says,

Now the big hand is on the **twelve**
and the little hand is on the **eight**.

Daddy says,
"Solomon, we have no time left!"

"Let's put on your **sweater** . . .

gloves . . .

and . . .

hat.

Now your **boots** and **raincoat**.

Who's all dressed and ready to go?"

ME!